PEDRO'S PICKLES
and the
AMERICAN DREAM

PEDRO'S PICKLES *and the* AMERICAN DREAM

DAVID A. EK

This is a work of fiction. Names, characters, places, and incidents are either the product of the author's imagination or used fictitiously, and any resemblance to actual persons, living or dead, business establishments, events, or locales is entirely coincidental.

Published by:
Badwater Books
Catlett, Virginia

Editing: Jim Pownall of Amy Scott Editorial, Kristy Phillips, and David Aretha.
Book Design: Creative Publishing Book Design
Cover Illustration: Bogdan Maksimovic

ISBN Paperback: 979-8-9876517-0-4
ISBN eBook: 979-8-9876517-1-1

Printed in the United States of America.

To the dreamers of the world.
May we all find camaraderie, comfort, and
solace somewhere down pickle farm lane.

1

A poor, overworked, and bedraggled farmer limped into the local cantina and chose the closest of its many empty tables. His threadbare overalls hung loosely on skin and bone bronzed by too much sun, too much sweat, and too much of never the right things. His day's weariness settled into his favorite chair, patron-polished by too much seated use and too many attempts to remember different times. Later, after several cañas, he began opening up to the tall, gray-haired camarero about how hard it was nowadays to make a living in the boreal savannah.

"It's hard," he said, "harder than the wood from a quebracho tree. Each generation is supposed to have it easier than those before, but they don't. If anything, it's worse." After more cañas, and a few La Negras on the side, the farmer confessed he pined for the day he could immigrate to America—"the land of freedom and opportunity."

The camarero paused to scratch his drooping brow before pouring the sorry man his next drink. As he poured, paused, scratched, and poured some more, he said, "I've seen you here before—many times." He then pulled up a chair and sat next to his inebriated patron, his only patron. Looking straight into drooping eyes, the camarero asked, "Why do you want to move to America?"

The slouching farmer, still glistening from field sweat and caked dust, began waving his sunbaked arm across the table in a futile gesture to explain. The farmer's wild gyration caused the caña to spill on the table. It slowly dribbled onto his lap. Ignoring the spill and his moistening, tattered clothes, the troubled farmer turned to his newfound camarero friend.

As he waved his arm across the cantina's bare walls in yet another futile gesture, he said, "I want, I need, a better life than this." As his hand settled back on the now-empty glass, he asked the camarero, "Wouldn't you?"

The Guaraní farmer whiled away his few idle moments in the cantina in a futile attempt to wash away the acrid taste of defeat and to drown out the plummeting sound a soul makes as it hits rock bottom. Over time, the cantina became the farmer's best friend and place of solace. As such, the two spent a lot of time together—alone.

As the camarero wiped the farmer's sweat and drink off the table and onto his sharply pressed bar apron festooned with sewed-on Paraguay flag patches, he paused before his measured words. "My friend, let me tell you a story about Pedro." After reflection, the camarero got up to bring the farmer a different drink. He returned with a fruity mixture. "Here's a tereré to soothe your worried mind—it's on the house." The weary farmer sat upright—a small price for free drinks. "Now, you see, I never met Pedro, but once, a long time ago, I met a friend of a friend—a childhood friend. He introduced me to Pedro and his family while sitting at the very spot you're sitting now. So, my Gran Chaco friend, let me share what I know about Pedro."

"Does that mean you'll refresh my tereré?"

"Sure, my friend. We treat you good here," the camarero said as he relished the opportunity to tell his favorite story once again.

As the camarero refilled the farmer's yerba mate cup, he also filled the cantina's smoky air with Pedro's story. It is not like the cantina hadn't heard passionate

Pedro stories before—it had, many times. However, this bedraggled farmer had not. So, the farmer, nursing his cold yerba mate cup, sat back and began listening to the story the best he could, considering his inebriated state.

Every night, beads of sweat ran down the temples of little Pedro's parents. They didn't know how their four Guaraní boys could make it on the Chaco Plain. Their four eldest had learned by an early age how to protect themselves, but not their eternally childlike and innocent Pedro. Chaco was rough for anyone, mestizo and Guaraní alike, but the family knew it would be especially rough for their poor Pedro—poor, naïve Pedro. "He is such a wisp of a boy," his parents often told one another privately. Their heart sank with the thought of what would become of little Pedro of the Chaco Plain. They would not be there forever to protect him, and his no-good brothers wouldn't likely help. Nor would the new people sweeping across the savannah, bringing with them change. Hard change. They knew Pedro needed a safe and trouble-free place to grow up to be a good, strong, and independent man. Their seven generations on the Chaco Plain needed to end with Pedro.

His parents had hoped his mandatory one-year military service would harden and prepare him for life, but it was not so. They'd hoped his independent brothers would help guide Pedro into the realities of life on the Chaco Plain, but they had their own problems dealing with the changes. And they had their own lives to worry about. *They are not going to be there for Pedro*, his mother and father often thought. It may have been too late for their older sons, but they still held hope for Pedro.

"What are we to do with Pedro?" his mother often asked, late in the evening in the quiet of their modest home under the star—and worry-filled Chaco Plain nights. His father had no answer either. However, they both knew that their savannah nights had become long, oh so long, oh so long.

Pedro's parents once had money, and their nights were not quite so long. For a while, they had money, influence, and a spacious bungalow—much more than most Guaraní within the Chaco Plain Boreal region could say. Over time, bad luck and corrupt officials bled their savings dry—and with it, their influence. Times had certainly changed on Paraguay's Chaco Plain, and it wouldn't get better soon. They had to find a way to give Pedro a better life and a new opportunity.

One day, they reached a desperate decision. They would give Pedro most of their remaining money and send him to America—the land of the free and the land of opportunity. The land where character mattered, not whether you were a peasant, had political influence, or were a mestizo from Captain Pablo Lagerenzá or a Guaraní peasant from an outlying village. Yes, they decided, Pedro had to leave for America at once.

Despite rumors and stories told by others, and retold again many times over, no one knew how he made it through South America, Central America, and Mexico alone. It must have been a horror-filled spectacle.

"How did he make it?" people frequently asked. "How did he endure the dangers and loneliness?" Nothing, even when he was an army courier, came close to preparing him for the hazards of immigrating to the United States.

Even more remarkable, the trip hadn't hardened him. He was still the same Pedro. Rumors circulated that as soon as he crossed the American border, Pedro got on bent knees and kissed the dust. While still kneeling and gazing into the deep-cobalt Texan sky, a vision of Saint Aloysius de Gonzaga crossed his mind in full radiant glory. Pedro immediately took this as a good omen—America had welcomed him to his new home. Pedro had finally, finally arrived.

What Pedro wanted above all else, other than to ensure the safety of his family and friends he left on the Chaco Plain, was for Americans to accept him as an American. He wanted and needed this, not only for himself but to honor his mother and father because they had sacrificed their comfort and security to give Pedro this once-in-a-lifetime chance.

Pedro bowed his head and prayed softly, "May Saint Gonzaga give me strength."

Every night, when wanting to stay clear of the Rio Grande corridor and the Border Patrol agents, he turned right at the setting sun. Throughout the journey, Pedro had time on his mind. Early thoughts drifted toward his military training and courier duties. Later thoughts focused on his dream of becoming an American. It was this dream, and duty to his parents, that drove him north.

2

Pedro lost track of the days, nights, kilometers, and other metrics left behind in his former reality. Each setting sun brought a new dawn more glorious than the last. Pedro began taking a ritualistic deep breath at the start of each morning. He filled his lungs with American air to better smell and taste the American experience. It was on one of these lung-filling pre-dawn mornings that Pedro found himself entering a new land, a place foreign to him, where Spanish dagger yuccas merged with overgrazed ear muhly and burrograss prairies. Around the next corner, Pedro came upon a desolate scene. His heart stopped. His eyes swelled. He exhaled.

Pedro's organs fought for primacy. Oxygen-rich blood surged through pulsating arteries. Tears evaporated into clear skies. Muscles froze as he gazed motionless upon the moonlit raggedness. Memories of the Chaco Plain and mental images of the past and present synced with the distant lightning roiling across flat-topped hills covered with grass and a scattering of live oak and persimmon. The entire scene culminated in one heavy sigh that drifted inward and lodged deep within the Guaraní's Texas-size heart and soul.

Pedro's single word said it all: "Home."

Just then, as a lightning flash illuminated a rocky hillside, right beyond the reach of the nearest moon shadow, he saw his future farm. His mind became alert. Memories and moistened eyes flashed back and forth. The dizzying signal reached his parched and ragged lips as they uttered what his mind commanded: "This will be my farm—an American farm all my own. All my own." As a boy back on the Chaco Plain, Pedro had helped his uncles on their farm. *But here, deep in West Texas, this will be my farm*, Pedro mused. *My farm.*

This particular ear muhly and burrograss-covered stony hillside deep within Texas's Pittsylvania County was *not* what experienced farmers would consider as being good farmland, but Pedro had his reasons. Some stories claimed Saint Aloysius de Gonzaga spoke with him that night. Other versions said it came from Pedro's inner

Guaraní—a mind and backbone as strong as a quebracho tree. Some people need to let passion and emotion guide them over logic and reason. Pedro was such a man. Regardless of the motivation, with confidence that Pedro never knew he had, he vowed right there and then to build a farm and home on that rocky hillside. He would build a home—*his* American home.

Leaving that stark, moonlit hillside behind, Pedro explored Pittsylvania to see what it had to offer. As Pedro strolled left of the rising sun, out into the hinterlands somewhere west of the Llano Plateau, he asked himself, *Where do people around here live?* After walking for a few kilometers in the warming morning air, the answer came to him: Pedro had arrived in the county's largest town. Before Pedro walked into Rose, it had a population of 227. After that watershed moment, it was 228.

Rose is a small town by American standards, but it is a well-known understanding that nothing is small in Texas. To the good, gun-toting citizens of Rose, the town is as big as Texas and as large as it ever needs to be. Next to God and family, Rosarians like traditions above all else—good West Texan traditions—and in that, Rose is truly a fittingly large Texan town.

Pedro lingered to take it all in. Grinding street sounds mixed with children's laughter took him to the sweetness of faraway places and fond memories. Someday, Pedro dreamed, his grandchildren would feel a moment this vivid for themselves—just like his first impression of the lovely town of Rose. Pedro had never seen so many busy streets. There were smiling people everywhere and driving about.

Pedro said, "Not even the Chaco Plain is as wonderful."

The once-slouching Paraguayan farmer sat erect on his moistened stool and blurted out to the camarero, "Why you tellin' me this? I dunno Pedro."

"Maybe you should, my friend," said the camarero. "Might just keep you safe. Might just make you happier."

As the farmer began slumping again, he waved for another caña. The camarero poured the drink and continued telling Pedro's story to the empty cantina. It is, after all, a camarero's job to watch after his customers' needs, or, in this case, the only customer's. With that, he continued telling Pedro's story to the needing farmer.

The only thing Pedro knew about farming was that he knew nothing about farming. He needed help. Pedro could speak only a few words of broken English. Guaraní would be of no use in Rose, Texas. Deep down in his heart, Pedro knew that to truly fit in with Americans and be accepted as an American, he would need to learn English. As Pedro strolled into Rose, he decided on two things: to learn English and the American way of farming—not how a Guaraní or mestizo farms, but an American.

With that foremost on his mind, Pedro walked tall and proud into Rose's corner store, The Yellow Rose. Pedro overheard two guys talking louder than southern screamer birds. They argued over the new resort an international corporation planned to build outside town. No matter where Pedro went, everyone had their own thoughts and opinions on the corporation—it was the talk of the town. Pedro would soon learn that in small American towns, word travels fast.

As Pedro approached his soon-to-be friends within the heart of The Yellow Rose, his heart raced faster than a jararaca strike. Pedro stopped to check that his clothing didn't look too ragged or unkempt. Images of his mother flashed through his mind. "First impressions are important," Mamá always said.

Pedro remembered these words and whispered them to himself. Outside, a fierce dust devil swirled past and disappeared into the hot Pittsylvania County summer. Pedro sighed. He shook the remaining dust out of his hair and stepped beyond the oaken door. He took shallow steps toward the shopkeeper.

With the best English he could muster, Pedro said, "Hello, sir! I Pedro. Farm, I buy. Farmer, are you?"

The elderly shopkeeper had lived his whole life in Rose. He never cared much for strangers, especially foreigners. With his small cockroach eyes, through oversized spectacles, he glared at the scrawny foreigner taking up his floor space and babbling incoherently.

Pedro did his best to read the shopkeeper's facial expression so that he could communicate with the American. However, the shopkeeper's vacant stare proved difficult for Pedro to read.

Once again, he stammered, "I Pedro. Hello."

With a grin he tried to conceal, the shopkeeper sneered at Pedro. He pointed a bony finger toward Jim, the well-fed, middle-aged, balding man doing nothing on a nearby oaken bench other than twirling his cream-colored Stetson hat. Pedro figured this balding man must be a farmer. Excited to meet his first American farmer, Pedro headed over to introduce himself.

"Hello, I Pedro. Farmer, are you?"

Jim looked down at Pedro and down at his Stetson before pivoting to glare at the shopkeeper. Pedro didn't pick up on Jim's not-so-subtle hint that he didn't like his sacred, and usually honored, idle bench time interrupted. He knew the shopkeeper sent Pedro over to him on purpose.

"Hello, I Pedro. Farmer, are you?" Pedro said again.

"I heard you the first and the second time!" Jim bellowed. "I'm not buying anything, so why don't you just run along back to where you came from."

"I Pedro." Pointing outside, he added, "Pedro home."

Standing strong and proud, using the best English he could muster, Pedro said a phrase he had practiced all the way from the Chaco Plain: "My dear fadder wanted give me good American life. He give me money to buy American farm. Do you know where Pedro buy American farm?"

For some unsaid reason, upon hearing Pedro's practiced words, Jim perked up and became attentive. The shopkeeper's grin grew wider as Jim rose, straining his already-tight leather belt with its turquoise-inlaid Texas-size buckle. Once Jim steadied himself and adjusted his mid-rib to its new gravitational position, he stuck out a welcoming hand to a wildly grinning Pedro.

"Hello, I'm Jim. Pittsylvania County's farm expert. I just know we will be the best of friends. I'm glad to meet such an industrious young man as yourself. What is your name, son?"

"What? Pedro not know what you say. I Pedro from Paraguay. I be American farmer."

"Of course you are," Jim said, twirling his grease-soaked Stetson between his stubby fingers. "I could see that from my bench. Even people over in the chicken supplies could see that. That's why I came over, to speak to you farmer to farmer."

"I no farmer, I Pedro. I hope to be farmer someday. Have you farm job? Pedro learns fast."

"Peppy—"

"Pedro."

"Whatever. I'll tell you what—I like you. I'm gonna do you a *big* favor. You'll never become a true American farmer by working as a hired hand on someone else's farm. You need a farm of your own. If you have cash, I can let you have a really good farm for one-half price. Whad'ya say, Peppy? I need to know now because I have other real Americans just waiting to become farmers themselves. I can't put them off forever. That wouldn't be American of me—right? So, Peppy, do we have a deal?"

"Pedro. I Pedro."

"Whatever."

"What kind farm?" asked Pedro.

"It's any farm you want it to be because *you* would be the farmer. *You* make the decision as an American farmer. It could be potatoes, peppers, parsley, potash, or pickles for all I care. The point is, it'll be *your* farm. You decide."

After a long pause, Pedro stared at the dusty wooden floor. He then looked up, smiled, and mumbled, "Pickles?"

"Yeah, yeah. I was only talking. You can grow anything you want on your farm, but if you want pickles, go for it. It'll be your farm, your decision."

"Americans like pickles, no?"

Jim turned to the shopkeeper. "Hey, Simon. Peppy here wants to know if Americans like pickles. I think he wants to buy a pickle farm. Do you want to tell him?"

Simon did not attempt to conceal his laughter. He shouted, "Sure, sure! You know better 'n anyone around here, Jim, that I can't keep enough pickles stocked. We Americans love pickles. If I had 'nuff money, I'd buy me a pickle farm and leave this shithole store behind. Sure, we love pickles!"

Jim wiped the grin off his well-fed face. With a serious tone rarely squeezed from his puffy cheeks, he said to Pedro, "There you go. And as luck would have it, the farm I mentioned I have for sale just happens to be a pickle farm. You can now have your very own pickle farm. Say, how much cash did you say you have?"

Pedro just stood there and stared.

"Do you want a farm or not?" Jim asked.

"Yes, Pedro want American farm."

"How much money do you have? How much money do you have to buy an American farm?" Jim scowled.

"Pedro keep little for food and stuff. Left, Pedro have seventy million guaraní. Is enough for farm? No?"

"What the hell is a 'gwaney'?"

"Guaraní."

"Whatever."

"Paraguay money."

Turning to the shopkeeper, who had been listening to the whole conversation, Jim said, "Hey, Simon, quick, look up on the internet how many greenbacks equal seventy million gwaney. I think it's Paraguay's dollar."

It took Simon several minutes to find the exchange rate for gwanies, but eventually, he broke the silence and said, "About ten thousand dollars."

Confused by the conversation, Pedro asked again, "Is enough for farm? No?"

"This is your lucky day," said Jim. "I have the perfect farm for you that just happens to be selling for exactly seventy million gwanies. How lucky could you be to come by at this very moment? Soon you will have both money and pickles. Is that seventy million in cash? If the resort ever comes into town, the land will sell for more than seventy million gwanies. I'd act fast on such a sweet deal if I were you. You did say cash, right?"

"I bring in American dollar. Three days. Deal? No?"

3

The following day, with a smile broader than the one he had been wearing since arriving in Rose, Pedro took a bus into San Angelo to visit the Western Union office. It was the longest bus ride of his entire life. The bus was only half full, so Pedro chose the best window seat. While everyone else played with their phones, Pedro stared out the window at the America that unrolled before his eyes.

Pedro found the Western Union office easy enough, but getting inside was another matter. Pedro recognized the two men hanging outside on the bench by the door. While he had never met the individuals before, they reminded Pedro of guys back on the Chaco Plain who had convinced his brother to work for the local drug cartel. They also reminded Pedro of a few militia-type people he had come across while serving as a courier in the Paraguayan army. Pedro didn't need proficiency in any American language to recognize trouble when he saw it. Pedro swung widely to keep his distance from them as he slid into Western Union's front door.

By following his father's instructions, Pedro had no difficulty in collecting the money sent to him. After stowing the money in the bottom of his satchel, next to the Honeycrisp apples he had bought earlier at the fruit stand along the Concho River, Pedro stepped out the door to head back to Rose to find Jim.

Immediately after stepping through the door, Pedro's face hit the pavement, and something tugged on his satchel. He rolled over and saw the two "trouble" guys who were hanging at the door when Pedro entered.

"Sorry. Pedro not mean to bump in you," Pedro said while still lying there, wondering what else to say or do.

Pedro felt someone still tugging on his satchel. It was the stubble-faced one. He wore fatigues with a large sewn-on red flag with a blue cross and white stars. "What do you have in your bag, foreigner?" he said as he continued pulling on the satchel. But it was tied around Pedro's waist. Pedro's whole future as an American rested in that satchel, so he held on tight. Pedro broke the satchel free from the flag-wearing, stubble-faced guy and lunged to his feet, but the bald guy with an American flag tattoo grabbed him by the arm.

"My friend just asked you a question, foreigner. What do you have in your bag?" the bald, tattooed man said as the stubble-faced guy closed in.

"I bet it's money. You got money in your bag, don't you?" the bald guy said. "First you take my American job, now you take my American money."

"Yeah, leave it with us—foreigner," the stubble-faced guy said. "Go back to wherever you came from. We don't need your type here, taking American jobs. Go home."

Pedro kicked the bald, tattooed man in the shin as he swung his Honeycrisp-filled satchel directly into the stubbled face of the other. As soon as Pedro broke free, he ran as fast as he could. Pedro was never a fast runner, but his courier-experienced legs were more than enough to outpace the balding man. The flag-wearing guy had already doubled over, gasping for air.

Pedro continued running. He ran along the Concho River, through the plaza filled with statues, and all the way to the bus stop. He didn't want to wait for the next bus for his trip back, so he stuck out his thumb, attempting to hitch a ride.

Nearly a hundred cars and trucks passed by without stopping before a gray-haired lady driving an old Pontiac offered Pedro a ride. "Where are you going, young man?" the Pontiac driver asked.

"Rose. Do you know of Rose? Pedro live there."

"My, that's a nasty scrape you have on your chin and forehead. Do you want me to take you to the hospital?"

"No hospital. Pedro's fine. This happens all the time. I only need ride into Rose. Do you know Rose?"

"I know where Rose is," the Pontiac lady said. "I'm going to Del Rio. I can pass right through Rose. I'll give you a ride if you like."

"Yes, please, "Pedro said. "You very kind. Thank you."

Pedro stepped into the Pontiac and placed his satchel carrying his ten thousand dollars carefully between his feet, but he held the strap tight in his hand. A few kilometers and two stories later, Pedro reached into his satchel and pulled out one of the apples he had bought along the sparkling Concho River. After savoring that sight and memory, Pedro bit into the Honeycrisp—the loveliest piece of heaven he had ever tasted.

On the agreed-upon date and time, Pedro left his encampment two hours out of town and walked into Rose. It was the busiest place he had ever seen. People were shopping, walking, driving, parking, talking, hugging, and waiting. It was unlike anything he had seen on the Chaco Plain.

This is just like I imagined, Pedro thought. *If all American towns are as wonderful as this, I am truly in heaven.*

Pedro had no trouble finding Jim; he was on his bench doing nothing special. Wearing the biggest grin Texas had ever seen, Pedro handed over the entire satchel to Jim, minus the apple. The Honeycrisp would serve as Pedro's dinner later that night.

As Pedro gingerly placed the apple in his pocket, careful not to bruise it, Jim yanked out the stack of bills and began counting. After finishing with his many clicks and grunts, Jim turned to Simon and then Pedro and broke into a Texas smile. "It's all here—all ten thousand dollars," he said. "This will do. This will do nicely."

"Thank you, Mr. Jim. Papers, may I? Please?" Pedro asked, wanting proof of land ownership.

After securing a piece of paper from Simon, who had rustled it from behind the counter, Jim scribbled a short note using the largest writing that Pedro had ever seen—the letters almost filled the entire page. Jim handed the paper over and asked Pedro to sign.

Pedro held his new treasure close, as he would a newborn. To Pedro, it looked legitimate: for one, it had letters and marks so big, it had to be official. Pedro signed it and handed it back to Jim with a small letter *P* scribbled at the bottom of the paper.

"Well, son, you are now the proud owner of an American farm." Jim held out his right hand, wanting to shake on it.

Before shaking, Pedro asked, "You sign too? No?"

"That may be the way you do it in Brazil, but not here in America."

"No Brazil."

"Wherever. You are now an owner of a real American farm, Peppy."

"Pedro."

"Whatever."

Pedro scanned the paper for a second time, looked up at Simon, then turned back to Jim. He stared back and forth between the paper and Jim enough times for Jim to lose his customary used car salesman's grin. Pedro hesitated in silence because he didn't want to expose his ignorance by asking questions. Besides, he wouldn't have found the right American words even if he had spoken up.

Well, after Jim's grin faded into the vast West Texas sky, Pedro finally found his words. "No signature? Pedro want signature."

"That's not how we do things here in America. Do you want the farm or not?"

Pedro sheepishly said to himself, *No signature? Well, if that is how they do it in America…*

Without a signature or answers to unspoken worries, Pedro slowly walked out of The Yellow Rose, cradling his newly minted farm deed, guarding it against wind, sun, dust, crinkle, and smudge. He strode down Rose's dusty lanes without one grain of dust or one ray of sun touching his deed. *I now own my very own American pickle farm*, he said to himself. *Mamá and Papá would be so proud if they could see me now.*

Earlier that day, Pedro had set up camp six kilometers out of town, within a tight cluster of cane cholla, ocotillo, and Mormon tea. Now he packed his things and moved his bedroll to the cane cholla, ocotillo, and prickly pear on the steep slopes of his land—his soon-to-be pickle farm. According to Jim, if he worked hard, he "could have the biggest pickle farm in Pittsylvania County." Pedro vowed to work hard. Real hard. However, a couple of hours later, his smile faded upon realizing that he still knew nothing about pickle farming. For that, he decided to turn, once again, to his friend Jim.

The following morning, when the cane cholla still cast long shadows across the scrubland, Pedro began the long walk into town to find Jim. Pedro went straight to The Yellow Rose. After pushing the oaken door open, Pedro saw Jim twirling his Stetson while sprawled out on the ornately carved oaken bench.

"Mr. Jim. Pedro needs help with pickle farm. You help Pedro?"

Jim stopped playing with his Stetson upon hearing the boy's voice. He looked up and saw Peppy. "What do you need, son?"

"Help. How to start?"

"Start what?"

"Farming."

After thinking it over a moment, Jim surprised even himself by telling Pedro, "Sure, but give me a few minutes. I really have been enjoying both the morning and the bench. After more enjoyment and relaxation, I'll give you a ride to your farm and point out a few things. How's that, Peppy?"

"That nice, Mr. Jim. Thank you," said Pedro.

He stood alongside the bench, quiet and unmoving. This distraction reminded Jim of a British palace guard defending Buckingham Palace. Jim could stand only two minutes of Pedro's hovering stoicism. With a heavy sigh, Jim rocked onto his feet and barked at the overeager guard, "Enough already. I can't stand you looming over me—it's enough to ruin a good bench moment. Come now, let's take a ride out to your farm."

"Thank you, Mr. Jim," Pedro said, following him as they sauntered to the truck.

Jim was in no hurry to do Pedro a favor. Besides, it would soon be a hot day. *There's no use working up a sweat,* he thought. As they climbed into the truck, he regretted saying he'd help the little immigrant boy. "Hot days are perfect bench-warming times," Jim grumbled as he began the dusty drive. He almost turned back when he looked down at Pedro and saw him smiling broadly. *Why is the guy always happy?* Jim wondered through his scowl.

"Idiot," Jim said.

They fell into silence.

In less than an hour, the smile and scowl walked toward Pedro's hillside.

Tucked between grassy, flat-topped clay hills and ear muhly- and burrograss-covered slopes were a few remnant and isolated floodplain terraces. Jim stopped on one of the terraces, almost causing Pedro to bump into him. Jim turned and stared at Pedro as would an old dog at a baby pulling on its tail.

Jim broke the silence while standing on a rock—his voice bouncing off the surrounding cliff bands as his plump shadow splayed out across the scraggly terrace. Jim's radiant profile was as commanding as a statute, complete with a sun halo riding on top of a grease-smeared Stetson. In his booming voice, he said, "This is *real* America, Peppy. Don't you just feel it? This is the land, Peppy, where character matters, where a person is free to fulfill their destiny to their heart's content. This is not only America, Peppy, this is Texas. Texas, God's country." Pedro nearly dropped to his knees as Jim's words echoed across the future pickle patch. Nowhere before had he heard such a rousing speech as the one his friend, Mr. Jim, just gave while standing on his rocky pulpit. A small part of Pedro wanted to bow down to the omnipotent Texan farming king and mentor.

Despite Pedro not knowing anything about Jim, Pedro immediately took to him and held him up as *the* idealized American. Pedro's deifying Jim may have been mystifying to impartial observers since the guy's main accomplishment most days was butt-polishing an oaken bench. As for employment, Jim dabbled in many things. When he wasn't polishing benches, twirling Stetsons, or pontificating to Simon, Jim whiled away his time being Rose's self-appointed spiritual leader. He knew Rose and Rosarians well and had been a popular town fixture his entire adult life.

Simon once told Pedro that Jim had a wife back home. Pedro was unlikely to meet her, since being a church-going woman, she didn't often frequent benches, farms, or feed stores. She preferred to while away *her* time and nervous energy in servitude to church events, social gatherings, and charitable functions—none of which were likely to invite anyone other than a *true* Rosarian, especially any Pedro types.

Jim's booming voice brought Pedro back to his reality and his pickle farm questions. "It's here," Jim said. Here is where you want to start a farm." Jim pointed out a small patch of ancient floodplain to Pedro.

"Why here?" Pedro asked his master.

"The soil's better, and it's not a far walk," he said, while looking beyond the lower draw. "That's where you'll want to sink the well. Pickles take water." He pointed around in wild gestures. "If you dig a well there and terrace your soil, your pickle farm should do just right."

"That would be good. I want to grow many pickles. Americans like pickles—and you, Mr. Jim, can have Pedro's first pickle."

"Yes, yes, that'll be fine, Peppy. Once you finish the work I outlined, come over and see me again, and I'll order you some seedlings."

Pedro mulled over Jim's thoughts as he scooped up a handful of darkened soil from one of the terraces. The loam felt cool to the touch. Pedro rolled it back and forth in his hand. Crunching a handful gave off the pungent smell of good growing soil. How Pedro knew this, he did not know. There must be some deeply hidden farming gene in all of us, no matter how far removed from ancestral hunter-gatherer, whether in West Texas or the Chaco Plain.

As the dust from Jim's truck faded into the hills, Pedro began his work in earnest—he knew what needed to be done. There were retaining walls to build, irrigation pipes to lay, rocks to move, native plants to remove. Over the next few weeks, Pedro toiled harder than he ever had in his whole life, almost as much as his mother and father did back home on the Chaco Plain—certainly more than his brothers ever had. He dug a meager but functioning well. He moved rocks. Stacked rocks. Built rock terraces and collected rainwater from a Pedro-carved rock basin.

Despite harsh working conditions, by the end of autumn, his farmstead began to take shape and form. Only on the rarest days, under leaden Texan skies, did Pedro seek rest at his favorite shaded spot, under a persimmon tree that commanded a fine view. He often sat and watched vultures as they rode thermals rising high above the clay hills and scraggly slopes surrounding Pedro's little patch of terraced heaven.

Pedro planned to follow Jim's farming advice—without deviation. When he had completed the to-do list that Jim outlined, Pedro wanted to visit his best friend to buy some pickle plants for his carefully terraced but empty farm. So, late in the afternoon, while vultures circled high overhead, Pedro began the long walk into town.

Pedro found Jim without difficulty. Jim sat idle on his bench. Pedro's confidence in Jim's friendship and kindness knew no limits, so with few words spoken, with cracked and bleeding fingers, Pedro handed Jim five hundred dollars. He had recently picked up the cash from the Western Union in anticipation of this day. As Jim's plump little fingers counted the bills, Pedro turned to him and said, "Me purchase 108—What do you call them? 'Little pickle trees.'"

"I'll order them for you, Peppy," Jim said.

"Pedro."

"Whatever!"

4

A week later, just as he said he would, Jim brought over 108 bare-root pickle tree seedlings packed in plastic-wrapped, moistened straw. As soon as Jim left, Pedro tore into the cardboard packaging and created three separate piles, one for each of the three varieties of pickle plants. Pedro grabbed a shovel, and with tree sprigs in hand and a satchel over his shoulder, Pedro busied himself night and day grubbing into the terraced West Texan dust. He planted the seedlings into nice, tight parallel rows—sixty-six per hectare, or as Jim instructed, twenty-six per acre. After Pedro finished, despite back pain, sore shoulders, burned neck, and blistered hands, he smiled at his pickle trees and American farm.

Once they were planted, Pedro watered most of his pickle plants by gravity-feed from his meager well. He watered them until the well ran dry. For the remaining seedlings, Pedro could do nothing more than wait for the next rain. He prayed to Saint Aloysius de Gonzaga that rain would come soon.

A week later, Pedro still waited and prayed. He squeezed a little more life-giving sweetness from the well, but its meager flow still could not water all 108 seedlings at the same time. Thoughts of his newfound American friends softened his growing worry lines and furrows. He frequently thought about Mr. Jim's generosity and tried to imagine his life without him. It was during these quiet thinking times that Pedro felt the most American. During quiet moments, Pedro pushed worries aside and got more things done on *his* American farm. With his mind at ease, he took deep breaths of real-life American air, noticed the subtle smells of each American juniper species, and watched the vultures circle high overhead, guarding over Pedro and his farm.

The severity of the drought brought clarity to the harsh realities of farming. As Pedro watched dust devils swirling about his slowly withering sprigs, he knew he needed help soon. Before trudging back to town, Pedro prayed that Mr. Jim would show him the way out of the drought.

The oaken planks pulled on sagging wrought iron hinges as Pedro stood in the store's empty doorway. Fresh chicken feed odors stung Pedro's eyes as he scanned The Yellow Rose's interior, across an empty bench, past the aisles, to an empty checkout register. Customers browsed the aisles, but no one appeared to be working.

"Where is Mr. Jim?" Pedro asked the customers. "Where is Mr. Simon?" No one answered him. Like on the church pews or Rose's streets, everyone silently pulled away from Pedro—he believed out of respect. However, Pedro didn't have time for such ponderings; he needed to find his friends.

After two chicken-feed-odor-filled minutes, Pedro found Mr. Simon out back, helping a shaved-headed man load baling wire into his old pickup. Pedro patiently waited and watched. The bald man had a pair of hour glass tattoos above each ear, and he wore a black and greasy Lynyrd Skynyrd T-shirt that had seen better days. Since it had been an incredibly tiring walk into town, Pedro wanted to sit down, but sitting on Mr. Jim's bench didn't seem right. Instead, Pedro leaned on a wall next to more chicken feed bags. The smell of fresh popcorn from behind the counter made him hungry. He soon forgot his grumbling belly when a tall and thin sapling-built man came out the store's back door and began staring at Pedro. The pallet that Pedro retreated behind did nothing to block the sapling man's stare.

Is there too much dust on my face? Are my clothes too un-American? What am I doing wrong?

No matter how many times Pedro checked himself over, the sapling man didn't stop staring. Pedro wished for a stout oaken door to block the man's prying eyes, but he had only a squat pile of chicken feed bags. Before Pedro could find an escape, the sapling man darted into the back door. Curious, Pedro followed.

The sapling man rushing down the aisle whisked a cloud of chicken feed odors with him. He must have not found what he had sought since he rushed back to the loading dock. Although Pedro hadn't yet made it back, he overheard the sapling man blurt out to Mr. Simon, "Hey, that guy inside. Is that the Peppy foreigner Jimmy talked about?"

"That's him, but what's it to you, Harry?"

"Just wondering," Harry said as he strolled over to Pedro. He offered a big smile and outstretched hand. "Hello. My name is Harry Burgess. I'm a farmer from up north. Jim's a friend of mine, so that means I'm a friend of yours. I understand you're farming a corner of Jim's old land. What is it you grow?"

"I Pedro. I bought pickle farm from nice Mr. Jim. You know how grow pickles? No? Do you have farm I can learn on?"

Both Simon and Kyle stopped loading the baling wire to watch.

"No, I don't grow no damn pickles," Harry said. "I have a cattle ranch, but I grow a little sorghum and wheatgrass. I also have the largest pecan orchard in Pittsylvania County. Our friend Jim told me you paid cash to buy your pickle farm. Pickles, like pecans, are a good crop, but there's too much pecan and pickle poaching in these parts. So, unless you hire someone to pickle patrol twenty-four seven, it'll be a waste of time and pickles. They'll steal every one of your pickles out from under your nose before you even have time to blink."

"What do you mean? Pedro not understand."

"Have you ever heard of cattle rustling? That's where people steal your cattle. There's a lot of cattle rustling around here, and they wouldn't think twice about pickle poaching."

"Oh, Pedro did not think about that."

"Of course you didn't, but I'll tell you what. Since we're friends, I'll help you out. For a hundred dollars a month, cash, I will send my cattle patrol over to your farm, so you can rest easy that no one will harm your crops once you plant them."

"I dunno. I have few money left."

"How much money will you have left once someone steals your pickles before your first crop ripens? Nothin!

You'll be out everything and have nothing in return. A mere hundred dollars a month is worth peace of mind and security, isn't it?"

"If you say so. Maybe for a few months."

"Great. You won't regret it. I'll be out to your camp sometime next week to pick up your first payment." With their arrangement set, Harry Burgess, the strange sapling man, pushed open the oaken door and disappeared into the shimmering Texan heat.

Pedro approached Simon as soon as he finished loading the baling wire. "Mr. Simon, please forgive Pedro. I am looking for … Do you know where I can find Mr. Jim?"

"What am I, Jim's secretary? I don't keep track of him, and he don't keep track of me, so bug off! I got work to do."

"Forgive me, Mr. Simon, but this is important. Where is Mr. Jim?"

As Simon brushed past Pedro to attend to a line of customers at the checkout, he said, "He ain't here. He's out of town on business for a couple of days."

Kyle, overhearing the entire conversation, approached Pedro while holding out his hand. "Hello, I'm Kyle. I have a farm down the road a bit. Did I hear you bought a farm here in Pittsylvania County?"

"Yes, yes, I bought farm. I American farmer now."

"Did I overhear you correctly? What are you growing?" asked Kyle.

"Pedro bought pickle plants from Jim. Pedro to grow pickle farm."

"You don't say," Kyle said while scratching his head. "You don't say."

Pedro turned toward the heavy, sagging front door and began the long dusty walk back to his farm.

A few mornings later, as Pedro hauled water in a large metal bucket to give to thirsty pickle seedlings, Harry Burgess arrived, as promised. He came to collect the pickle patrol money—cash that Pedro had picked up the previous afternoon from Western Union. The exchange on this dry Texan morning involved few words, which suited Pedro and Harry just fine. Harry left Pedro's camp with a grin and one hundred freshly minted dollars in his pocket. Pedro's deeply furrowed face obscured any semblance of a smile. Perhaps it was the drought, the bleeding of his money reserves, or the dreaded need to return with the bucket for yet another one-kilometer trip to the stream, but he felt no satisfaction in being one step closer to his American dream.

Pedro's optimism began creeping back into his tired bones the following morning. Below the persimmon tree, Pedro rose from his bedroll and greeted the new day's sun and unlimited possibilities. In appreciation for such a fine day, he built a thatched lean-to. It provided welcoming shade on especially hot afternoons.

Pedro started attending Sunday church services to solidify his place in his new home and community. To Pedro, this seemed right as rain since real communities shared their religious devotion amongst themselves. Despite such efforts and overtures, Pedro still felt held back from full acceptance due to his limited English. However, fellow Rosarians showed their respect through nonverbal ways. For instance, as Pedro decided which church pew to sit on each week, everyone grabbed their purses and jackets and cleared the way for Pedro.

Aren't they kind? he thought on more than one occasion.

Although Pedro didn't mind sitting close to others, it warmed him so to think Americans cared for him that much. Back on the Chaco Plain, Pedro had blended in. No one noticed him. However, everything here was different. Even when walking down the streets of Rose, strangers paid Pedro respect by clearing the street and crossing the sidewalks for him. Complete strangers went out of their way so as not to crowd him. *How thoughtful.*

One afternoon following church, Pedro's mood began to worsen. The seedlings were in poor shape without any rain and with the well only half-producing—Pedro didn't need Jim to tell him that. Also, they looked different than he had imagined. While Pedro had never seen a pickle tree seedling before, he imagined them to be stout enough to hold pickles. Maybe the drought withered them, but the wispy seedlings couldn't have held a single one, let alone a whole crop. Pedro shrugged these concerns off. Jim said wait, so Pedro told himself, "Patience, Pedro, patience."

Days turned into weeks, and weeks turned into two months. Some drizzle came, and some trees grew, but no pickle buds set, and no pickle fruit grew. Pedro wondered what had gone wrong. It was around then that he began to have visitors. The good people of Pittsylvania County heard about Pedro's farming struggles. Word of Pedro and his pickle farm had spread far and wide. They didn't come to help. Pedro and his pickle farm were mere curiosities—and a source of gossip around town. Pedro had visitors nearly every day. The only thing in Rose that spread faster than talk was gossip.

Regardless of the real reason they came to visit, Pedro couldn't be prouder. He liked showing his farm to new friends, and he took it as a sign that Americans were accepting him as one of them. He wrote home to tell his mother and father, but the letter returned undelivered.

Over time, the curiosity visits dried up faster than the pickle farm's well. Pedro continued hauling water and tending thirsty trees as best as he could, but it tore on his mind, body, and health. When real rain finally came, it was as if nature tried to make up for the lost time. The booming black hammer-headed demigod rose to gothic and mythic proportions—and then it burst. The deluge ravaged large swaths of Pittsylvania County. Little Pedro could do nothing to protect his pickle plants against the onslaught. Pedro wrapped himself in his rain-soaked bedroll and huddled under his thatched lean-to. There was nothing else for him to do other than hold on tight to the strained lean-to pole and pray it wouldn't be a long night.

As dawns often do, daybreak brought a cleansing smell to the land and water that all but humbled the remaining dazed and confused survivors. The storm transformed the draws, canyon, and floodplain oxbows into something new. The storm changed more than mere landforms. Throughout Pittsylvania County, death and despair hung in the air and crept along blocky ridges, into deep-green forest glens, and throughout Rose's muddy brown streets.

Does Mr. Jim need any help? was the first thought that crossed Pedro's mind as he tepidly crept into the morning's stillness. He needed to find out, so Pedro began the long walk to Jim's place.

As Pedro soon learned, Jim's storm damage was not as bad as many other homes throughout the region. While a flood damaged parts of Jim's pecan orchard, the worse damage was to his cattle. Jim was missing over ninety cows. Jim had sent all his employees out to search for missing livestock. By the time Pedro arrived, all search parties had returned empty-handed. Jim was too busy to talk to Pedro, so Pedro took the initiative to head out alone, on foot, to search for Jim's missing livestock.

I need to think like a cow, Pedro thought as he searched canyons and draws that Jim's employees likely had never set foot in before. Since Pedro arrived in Pittsylvania County, his footsteps had graced most nooks and crannies the county offered. During these many wanderings, Pedro often came across Jim's livestock—many times far from any roads. *Mr. Jim's people likely didn't get out of their cars*, Pedro thought as he continued to think like a cow.

Six hours later, Pedro found sixty of Jim's missing cattle; forty-three were still alive, but injured. Floodwater had swept them away, injuring many and confusing all. Pedro walked back to Jim's place and let the foreman know the location of the stranded and lost cattle. Pedro could do no more on his end, so he walked back home to assess the storm's damage to his pickle farm.

Miraculously, Pedro's farm suffered little damage from the Big One. Pedro's strong and sturdy rock-lined terraces had held against the storm's onslaught. *Saint Aloysius de Gonzaga watched over me and my farm*, Pedro thought as he cleaned up the minor damage brought forth by that dark night.

A few days later, a terrible sickness came upon Pedro. He doubled over in pain and fever. He could no longer work the fields. With his remaining strength and force of will, Pedro dragged himself to the partial shade under the persimmon tree. He leaned against his friend's stout trunk, but with Pedro's high fever, the persimmon view provided no comfort. Pedro became acutely aware of his loneliness and isolation. He was in sorry shape, and he knew it. Still leaning against the persimmon, Pedro faded in and out of consciousness. One such bout took Pedro back to his family on a far, distant land—although it was his family, and this strange land was *not* the Chaco Plain or the savannah of his youth.

The smell of fear and death hung in the air as village families ran in all directions. His father grabbed little Pedro by the arm and led him toward the nearby forest. Pedro's little legs ran as fast as they could, but it was not fast enough.

Out of nowhere, a horse and rider descended upon the village and barreled down upon Pedro and his mother and father. Suddenly, his family disappeared, and all Pedro could see was a horse and rider looming over him, blotting out the entire sun. The rider drew a sword from its sheath. Left, right, back, and forward—Pedro's eyes flicked, but Mamá and Papá were nowhere to be found. Little Pedro was about to face the swing of the warrior's sword all alone. As soon as he twisted away, Pedro heard the blade's hiss as it sliced through the air. He ran—only to come face-to-face with the horse's sweaty sheen and fire-red flanks. Using a force of will he didn't know he had left, little Pedro faced the redness. As he caught his breath and bravely stood his ground, Pedro caught sight of his village in the distance, engulfed in flames. All he could do was stare—and wonder what had just happened.

That pause did not last long before the flame-red horse and mount were fast upon little Pedro. Still, he remained transfixed, feet firmly planted on earth, and eyes upon the flickering remains of his former world and all he knew. Immediately before the red *was upon him, some force yanked Pedro out of the way. He looked up and saw it was Papá, with Mamá standing right behind.*

This was only a momentary save since the horse and mount, now more enraged than before, turned and were quickly after them. There were no more surprises this time. They were truly alone.

The redness pounced. There was no other choice. Pedro's father pushed his son aside as his mother shouted, "Run, Pedro! Run to the trees. If you love me, run—run!" With that, his mother and father jumped upon sweaty flanks and clawed deep into the redness. They knew, for them, it was futile, but it bought Pedro a few seconds.

Pedro ran as fast as he could until he reached the tree line. Under cover of the first quebracho tree, Pedro turned to see the glistening redness of the horseman's sword being brought down upon his mother and father, instantly killing them both.

In the flickering glow of the town's remaining embers, the horseman rode off, leaving Pedro's parents lying as motionless as Pedro's spent legs. Nothing and nobody moved. The only thing Pedro mustered was a whimper. He was about to pass out, but the spirit of his motionless Mamá and Papá gave Pedro strength and purpose as they spoke in unison to their son, "For heaven's sake, our sake—survive!"

5

As he opened his eyes, Pedro felt the warmth of the West Texan sun on his face. Sweat ran down a reddened cheek and into his open mouth. Turning to gain his bearings and composure, he managed only a groan. After a second attempt, Pedro saw he must have rolled out of the coolness of the persimmon's welcoming shade and exposed himself to the afternoon's full sun. He pulled himself back to lean against the trunk of his comforting friend. As he leaned against the persimmon, Pedro thought about his parents and their home on the Chaco Plain. *Was the nightmare an omen? Are Mamá and Papá safe? The drug gangs I heard about—did they enter my home village? Did they burn Mamá and Papá's home?*

Despite leaning calmly under full shade, Pedro began sweating again. *Am I all alone now?* He sat there thinking, worrying. Sweat dripped from his eyebrows and disappeared into the thirsty dust. As Pedro shook the disturbing vision out of his head, his eyes caught the motion of a passing stranger who had come into sight.

Sharon left Minnesota four months earlier, wanting to travel and see the country—to experience the true nature of America and its people. She thought about becoming a Peace Corps volunteer in some far-away overseas community in need, but opted instead for getting a better sense of her own community, her brothers and sisters—the American people. Being a restless and idealistic college dropout, she thought the open roads and byways would teach her more about people and truth than any college course could ever accomplish. So, she and Charley—her seven-year-old Saint Bernard—took to the open road. With her thumb out, she hitched rides and headed closer to Maine. She likened their adventure to Steinbeck's *Travels with Charley in Search of America*, which she kept a copy of tucked into her knapsack. She spent a few weeks watching moose, and meeting and spending time with the locals around Mount Katahdin before hitching to West Texas via Appalachia, Key West, and the Gulf Coast.

She hadn't planned to go to Rose or visit Pedro. She didn't even know of their presence. Steinbeck hadn't once mentioned the town. Rose and Pedro were just chance encounters during her search for the American soul. With that in mind, she may as well have sought out Pedro and Rose since they represented more than just a mere snippet of Americanism. They could have been the subject of a college-level sociology class, but since Sharon dropped out of college, fate may have led her to the *real* Rose. However, Sharon chanced upon Pedro long before arriving in any quirky West Texas town beyond the outer margins of the Llano Plateau.

As blonde-headed Sharon, in her breezy soy fabric eco-wear, strolled down an isolated and primitive Pittsylvania County back road, she saw in the distance a persimmon tree. When she was young, her father told her lovely stories of persimmon trees. As such, she grew fond of this often neglected, derided, and unwanted farmstead invader. The last persimmon she saw had been weeks before and far to the east.

The persimmon tree's distinctive shape materialized as she and Charley slowly walked toward it. Memories of her father's persimmon stories flooded Sharon's mind. What also emerged as they drew closer was something slumped under the tree.

"Is that a dead body?" she hesitantly asked Charley.

Charley wanted to pull forward, but Sharon held back. As usual, Charley won, so they ran and trotted to have a closer look. As they drew near, the limp and wasted human-shaped lump began to move. It had a head, and it turned toward Sharon just as Charley came up and licked Pedro's sweating forehead.

"Oh my God! Are you okay?" Sharon shouted as Charley continued licking Pedro's face. At first, Pedro responded neither to question nor saliva.

After her third attempt to get a response, Pedro gently pushed Charley aside and asked, "Who are you? What are you doing? Where am I?"

"My name is Sharon. I am here to help. And you are on a bare, rocky hillside somewhere far west of the Llano Plateau."

"Thank you. Hello. I am Pedro. I am not feeling very well. If I may trouble you, may I have some fresh water?"

"Sure, Pedro, sure," she said as she rummaged through her knapsack for water and food. She found and offered him a water bottle.

In a manner of seconds, Pedro drank the entire contents. While handing the empty bottle back, Pedro said, "Pedro still thirsty. Water. More, do you have?" After downing one more bottle, Pedro leaned onto the persimmon tree, and he and Sharon began talking. They talked like they were fast friends.

Sharon stayed with Pedro throughout the afternoon, the next, and into the third. Being on foot and without a cell phone, Sharon had no means to call for help. Pedro needed tending, and Sharon would never abandon a person in need. Besides, the two of them shared an unspoken understanding and trust. They needed few words to communicate, for they took to each other right off. To Sharon, Pedro was one of the faces of America that she hoped to meet on her journey. She planned to stay a few days helping Pedro recover. *Besides, you can't know someone by just saying "hello,"* she thought as she and Pedro talked and talked under the comforting shade of the persimmon tree. To Pedro, Sharon seemed like a person he had known for years.

During his more lucid moments, Sharon told Pedro stories to keep his spirits up. She expected no response but thought just hearing a human voice would help. The persimmon tree that Pedro leaned against inspired her first story.

On a faraway distant land once stood a grand garden filled with all sorts of delicious fruit. People came from far and wide to visit the grove and taste its sweet bounty. Off to the side of this luscious garden was a persimmon grove that few people noticed. Visitors to the lovely fruit grove occasionally asked the gardener why she didn't cut down the persimmons and plant better trees with sweeter-tasting fruit.

The gardener said, "I could never do that. I love the deep claret-red color of the autumn fruit, and I also enjoy eating it."

One visitor scrunched his face and said, "I heard persimmon fruit is bitter, so why save a bitter fruit when you could have only sweet varieties?'

"You are right, they are bitter, but I still like them," she said. "They're wonderful. They are bitter only because they are high in tannic acid."

"I know about that," groaned Pedro as he rolled over upon hearing Sharon mention tannic acid. It reminded Pedro of quebracho trees and his home and family on the Chaco Plain. "Pedro know about tannic acid. Papá taught me," he said while pulling in closer to Sharon to hear the rest of her story.

"Yes, tannic acid is a binding agent. It helps hold the fruit firm so it doesn't fall apart." With that fact behind her, Sharon continued her persimmon story.

The still curious visitor said to the gardener, "But if it is bitter, why not just cut the persimmon down and plant a useful species?"

"Oh, because the delicious fruit are tiny bundles of Mother Nature herself," the elder gardener said. "They make good jams too. I cannot cut down persimmon trees—they are my favorite. Besides, there is nothing in nature that is useless."

"I would think bitter fruit is useless," said the visitor.

"Nothing in nature is useless," repeated the gardener.

"That is a nice thought," moaned Pedro, "but that is not what I have been hearing my whole life. But it makes a good story."

"Then they are ignorant and foolish people," Sharon said. "Do you want to hear another persimmon story? Are you up for it?"

"Yes, please," said Pedro.

Without missing a beat, Sharon continued entertaining Pedro with another persimmon story.

This is an old story about an old man, also on a land far away. On this poor man's farm stood a grand persimmon grove, but he didn't appreciate the trees. He began cutting them down so beneficial trees could grow in their place. The farmer needed money to properly care for his elderly father, who suffered badly from atherosclerosis—a serious heart disease. If I cut the persimmons down, I can use the space to plant useful species. Maybe someday I would be able to afford heart medicine for my ailing father, *the farmer thought as the first persimmon crashed to the ground under the farmer's axe.*

Just then, a traveling apothecary rushed up and shouted, "Don't cut persimmon trees down! They are much too valuable to use as firewood."

"I'm not using persimmon trees for firewood. I'm cutting them down because they are useless and a waste of space."

"What I would give to have a persimmon tree or two," said the apothecary.

"Whatever for?" said the farmer.

"Why, because persimmon fruit is the best treatment for people with heart ailments, ranging from coronary heart disease to atherosclerosis to arrhythmia."

"Did you say atherosclerosis?" the bewildered farmer asked, beads of sweat forming on his temple.

"Yes, persimmon fruit is the best medicine for many heart conditions, including atherosclerosis.

I'll tell you what; I'm always in short supply of persimmon fruit. How about if you save a few of your trees? That way, I'll purchase several bushels of persimmon fruit every time I pass by your farm. Persimmon fruit is worth its weight in gold to anyone with heart disease."

The farmer thought for a moment, then took the apothecary up on his offer. The farmer saved his persimmon trees and not only sold them to the apothecary whenever he passed through the area but also fed them daily to his ailing father. His father lived to a very ripe old age—all because the farmer began looking upon and seeing persimmon trees in a new light.

After ending her story, Sharon paused before talking again to an only half-awake Pedro. "My father liked those stories so much, he named me after the persimmon tree. In some parts of the country, persimmon fruit is called 'Sharon fruit.' So, you see, Pedro—you, your persimmon tree, and me—fate brought us together."

Pedro smiled and then began drifting into the half-awake and half-asleep stage in which dreams become most vivid and intense. To Pedro, the sweet, woody smell of persimmon fruit took him back to hot days and simpler times, sipping fruity yerba mate and tereré on the Chaco Plain. As Pedro's consciousness came and went, he noticed Sharon had been talking the whole time.

"My father always liked that persimmon story," Pedro caught her saying. "As a child, I heard it many times over and over. So, when I saw you sick and leaning against a persimmon tree, it brought back fond memories of my father." Turning and staring at the persimmon tree, she said, "Pedro, do you know how this persimmon tree got here? They aren't native to West Texas. Maybe it's an escaped ornamental, or perhaps an introduced transplant. Wherever it came from, it certainly provides you good shade, doesn't it, Pedro? If you hadn't been in the shade when I found you, I don't know what would have happened to you."

Sharon tended to Pedro's food and water needs the best she could, given she had an empty knapsack and empty pockets. She stayed with Pedro long enough for the fever to break and his condition to stabilize. She even one day walked out to get Pedro some help and supplies. If she stuck around long enough, Pedro promised her his farm's second pickle—the one after Jim's. Pedro asked Sharon for one more favor. Although weak, his mind was clear enough to release Sharon from any other obligation toward him beyond delivering a note to Jim.

"I need help to be better, but I don't want burden you no more—you have done much ready. If you please, deliver a message to my friend Mr. Jim. No? You find him on store bench in Rose."

"Sure, I'll deliver a note for you. Is that all? You were pretty sick. You must be weak. During your fitful fever-talk, you spoke nonsense about pickle plants and pickle poachers. I couldn't make sense of any of it. It must have been your fever talking."

"Yes, weak. I am weak. But my friend Mr. Jim help. After giving note to Mr. Jim, please go rest of your trip. Please!"

Sharon wrote while Pedro dictated. Once they had finished, she folded the note and placed it within the pages of her Steinbeck book.

6

Later that afternoon, Sharon and Charley headed down the road toward Rose. Sharon had no trouble finding Jim. He sat on his bench, twirling his greasy Stetson, just as Pedro had said he would. She not only hand-delivered the note directly to Jim, but she also emphasized the urgency of the matter. "Pedro's all alone," she said. "He's out of food and water and just got through a bad fever. He assured me you would help get him back on his feet."

"Yes, I'll take care of it immediately," Jim said. "Thank you, young missy."

"My name is Sharon," she retorted.

"Whatever," Jim said as he shuffled out of the store. "I'll take care of him—thanks!"

Sensing there wasn't anything more to do, Sharon continued her explorations of Americana on her slow drift toward Los Angeles. Had she known that Jim wouldn't do anything to help Pedro, she would have purchased supplies and returned them herself. Instead, she trusted the man Pedro trusted—she trusted Jim.

A few days later, Pedro began worrying that something had happened to Jim. He could wait no longer. It took him four times as long, but Pedro's sorry legs carried him into town. Throughout the journey, he fell several times but managed to get up and continue. Each fall took him longer to get back up, except when in view of townsfolk. *Come on, Pedro, get up*, he kept saying to himself. *Americans don't fall so easily.* Since Jim hadn't responded to his note, Pedro willed himself to come into town to see if his friend Jim needed help.

Pushing The Yellow Rose's heavy doors open, Pedro fell over again. He felt himself falling again when he saw the bench. "Where is Mr. Jim?" he said to the empty store. Pedro hadn't even the energy to find Simon. Instead, Pedro walked, fell, rested, and walked some more over to the butcher shop. Anna Maria, the butcher, had always been kind to Pedro.

Anna Maria grew up in Texas, not far from Big Bend country. She came from old Texan stock stretching back generations. She took to Pedro immediately. There was something about Pedro that reminded Anna Maria about her younger brother, thirty years ago, back when he was Pedro's age. It was partly this reason that, when no one watched, Anna Maria often slipped Pedro slabs of meat wrapped in waxed paper.

So after his ordeal and illness, in his weary state and with heavy legs, Pedro stumbled over to Anna Maria—he needed a friendly face and gentle kindness. Anna Maria almost fell over herself when she saw Pedro's condition. She rushed over and helped him into the back office. Once she got him sitting in front of the air conditioning, she gave Pedro a jug of water and a salad she had planned to have for lunch. Later, she also gave him a grilled rib eye steak. Pedro stayed with Anna Maria for a couple of days. During his recovery, she pulled Pedro aside and said, "Pedro, please be careful. You have a kind heart. I would hate to see you hurt. Not everybody in Rose is friendly. You may not want to hear this, but I've known Jim for twenty years. He's done a lot for the town, but there's that other side …"

"Mr. Jim has been wonderful. He is my friend. Not Mr. Jim," Pedro pleaded with a volume that rose to a crescendo.

Pedro's fear and desperation startled Anna Maria since she had never seen him so animated. "All I'm saying is to be careful. I care for you, Pedro."

"Thank you. You have been very kind. I thank you, but Mr. Jim is my friend."

Anna Maria left it at that. She believed if she pushed it anymore, Pedro might become angry for the first time in his life. *Imagine that*, Anna Maria thought. *Pedro getting angry.*

When he was ready to return to his farm, Anna Maria drove Pedro home with a carload of groceries and emergency supplies. She promised to stop by in a few days to check on him.

Being young, strong, and filled with hope and joy, Pedro soon returned to full health. A week later, he walked into town to thank Anna Maria and make sure Jim was okay. Before Pedro had a chance to thank Anna Maria, he saw Jim walking down the street. Pedro approached Jim to ask if he was feeling well. As soon as they began talking, Kyle, still wearing his well-worn Lynyrd Skynard T-shirt, rushed over to join the conversation. Ever since they had first met, Pedro had occupied many of Kyle's thoughts and even the rare idea. Kyle had also thought about Pedro the previous evening while watching the evening news.

After catching up with Jim and Pedro, Kyle blurted out, "Hey, kid. Remember me? I'm Kyle. We met at The Yellow Rose when I was loading baling wire."

"What do you want?" asked Jim, while contorting his face and pushing back his Stetson.

"This ain't about you, Jim. This is about my new friend." Turning to Pedro, he asked, "Do you remember me?"

"Yes. Pedro remembers. Hello, how are you, Mr. Kyle?"

"Yeah, yeah, I'm fine. I just heard last night on San Angelo's news about some crisis in Paraguay. Didn't I hear you're from Paraguay?"

"Yes, Pedro from the Chaco Plain in Paraguay. What you heard?" Pedro asked while stepping in closer to Kyle, still panting from his short jog.

"From what I heard, drug gangs are ransacking and burning towns and people throughout Paraguay. I think they said something about 'Waco Plane.' Whatever or wherever the hell is a Waco Plane."

"I am from the Chaco Plain. Mamá and Papá live there. Are they all right?" Pedro asked while stepping still closer to the still panting Kyle.

"Do you know if they were killed or not?" Kyle asked.

"That's not the way to treat my friend Peppy," scolded Jim.

"This ain't about you, Jim," said Kyle. "So butt the hell out."

Seemingly oblivious to Jim and Kyle's exchange, Pedro silently stood there, unable to form any words.

Kyle interrupted Pedro's reflection and concerns by offering unsolicited advice. "Pickle trees don't set buds unless the farmer self-pollinates using pollination powder. And I just happen to have a few cans back in my truck. See, bees can't pollinate pickles if they can't find your pickle plants. This is where my pollination powder comes in. If not, bees won't be able to find any pickle blossoms, and no pickles will set."

It took Pedro a moment for Kyle's latest words to set in, since his mind was elsewhere, on lands and people far away.

Figuring Pedro was slow in understanding English, Kyle repeated, "You need to buy some of my pickle pollination powder."

"I buy your pollination powder if could, but Pedro's money is gone," Pedro said. "No more satchels and no more Western Union. Need sell pickles first—even for food. Pedro is hungry, but still no pickles. Besides, I need to find out what happened to my family, to my mamá and papá."

"What choice do you have, you little …" Kyle's eyes pierced Pedro's, causing Pedro to look down and step back. Noticing Pedro's reaction, Kyle paused, and then he said in a soft, reassuring voice, "Listen, I didn't mean anything by that. Clearly, no one wants trouble. I certainly don't. The last thing you need is a bunch of Border Patrol agents snooping about. So, hey, why not take the easy way out and work with me?"

After a brief pause, as if Kyle attempted to work his little-used mind, he came upon an idea. He broke into a grotesque and contorted grin.

"I've seen that look before, Kyle—what are you up to?" Jim asked.

"You never mind, Jim, this is between me and my new friend," Kyle said while grabbing Pedro by the shoulder as they turned their backs on Jim.

With that, Jim said, "Whatever," and walked away.

"I can help you out there too," Kyle said. His grin shifted into a sneer, especially once Jim was no longer there. "I got fence work to do. I'll pay you for it, but I have eight miles of barbed wire fencing that needs replacing and repairing. It's long and hard work, but if you start at five tomorrow morning, I'll pay you a dollar an hour plus the remaining wages in pickle pollination powder. You won't get a better offer. You need pickle pollination powder, and I need my fence set—and neither of us needs the Border Patrol snooping about. So, it's a win-win, isn't it, Pedro?"

"I guess so," Pedro said. "You need fence, and I need powder. Pedro be there for fence work tomorrow."

Pedro worked long and hard, not just that day, but the next, and the next, and on to the third week. He learned many things useful for his own farm, but he also learned the hard way that it's not easy setting fence posts in rocky ground. But Pedro worked hard as he put a worker's pride into the fence. At the end of the project, Kyle admitted Pedro's fence work was the best he had ever seen. Pedro's Texas-size smile masked his slouching shoulders, sore back, and drooping eyelids.

After the fence work, Pedro had pollination powder *and* enough money for three weeks' worth of food. Kyle estimated Pedro's pickle pollination powder should last an entire year. While that might have been so, Pedro found his three weeks of food only lasted two. Furthermore, despite dusting all the pickle plants with pollination powder, his seedlings still hadn't set any pickle flowers.

During Kyle's next visit, after hearing Pedro had no more fence money left, he said, "I'll tell you what, Peppy. I'll help you out big this time. I have a friend who could use a person just like you, and he'll pay good money. You'll have enough for all the pollination powder and food you want and then some. So, whaddya say, should I call my friend Leonard?"

"What do I have to do?"

"What th' hell I know? Do you want to talk with Leonard or not?"

"So, you trust this Mr. Leonard?" Pedro hesitantly asked.

"I don't know. You need to make up your own mind, kid. I ain't your father."

Pedro wasn't sure how to answer. He needed the money, but something told him this wasn't right. While still thinking it over, Pedro felt his head nodding, but at the same time his feet told him to run far away.

Three days later, Leonard drove up in a restored and freshly painted shovel-nosed Firebird Trans Am—red as a cactus flower. Leonard stepped out and paused long enough to rub whatever dust had settled on his leather cowboy boots. He stepped toward Pedro in his thatched lean-to. It was no bigger than a bedroll.

"Are you the Peppy that Kyle talked about—the one needing a job?"

"Yes, I am Pedro."

"Pedro it is. I thought you were Peppy. Whatever. If you work out, I have an important job for you. It's not hard, but you must follow my directions and do exactly as I say—no Pedro changes and no Pedro thoughts. Only my thoughts, my directions, my instructions, and my words. Got it?"

"Pedro understand. What do you need me to do?"

"Three simple things. Requirement number one: you are to drop off one package every Monday to a little airstrip a few miles out of town. Place the package in an old wooden box hidden under a clump of trees. Do you understand requirement number one?"

"Yes, yes. Pedro understand. Please continue."

"Requirement number two: pick up another package in the grocery store parking lot late on Friday night from a person who goes by Fred. Now, who do you give the package to?"

"Mr. Fred. Pedro understand."

"Good. Now the last, but most important, requirement is: don't talk or say anything about this job or me—to nobody! Got it?"

Pedro nodded. "Pedro is to take package to airplane box. Pick up another package from Fred at food store. Pedro is not to tell anyone about nothing. Pedro is honest. If you say don't tell anyone about job, I won't tell. I won't tell anyone."

For these three tasks, Leonard offered Pedro nothing useful for a farm, let alone a pickle farm. He didn't have powder, plants, patrols, or whatnot. However, he offered him five hundred dollars a week. This was the kind of money Pedro never believed one person could ever earn or own—certainly more than anyone on the Chaco Plain ever had. Pedro steadied himself by grabbing the lean-to. He felt the American dream blowing hard upon his back as if God's breath was lifting him into the exalted heavens.

"Saint Aloysius de Gonzaga is smiling on me today," Pedro said. *All this money for only three simple things*, he thought. *It doesn't seem right.*

Pedro thought, *This is the easiest job ever—and so much money. If Mamá and Papá could see me now. They would be so proud.*

For Pedro, the work was embarrassingly simple. All he did was move packages from one location to another. *This was even easier than my courier work in the army,* Pedro often thought.

Shortly after his first five-hundred-dollar payday, Pedro went into Rose to pay Anna Maria back for all the food and care she had always provided him. "That's very thoughtful of you," Anna Maria told Pedro, but she didn't accept a single penny. Instead, she sent Pedro away with another free bag full of meat trimmings and special cuts wrapped separately in waxed paper. Before heading back home, Pedro used some of his easily earned new money on bulk food that could be stored without refrigeration.

After a few weeks and several five-hundred-dollar payments, Pedro ate better and began gaining back some of his lost weight. He had become so thin. Jim joked that Pedro, from the side, blended in with the scraggly pickle plants. Pedro also had enough money to pay Jim, Harry, Kyle, and the other friendly neighbors for additional pickle patrols, pollination powder, weather insurance, and the required monthly pickle permitting fees.

Despite all the good news, Pedro smiled less frequently than he had just weeks earlier. His trees still had no pickles or pickle buds. According to Jim, the pickle season would soon end.

His pickle setbacks did nothing to still Pedro's proud patriotism for his new, adopted home. However, he often thought about family and friends back in his old home. Pedro had fond memories of the family sitting around the dinner table, eating soyo, telling each other stories, and sharing their hopes and dreams.

By candlelight, under a chilled black sky, Pedro pulled out his satchel and looked at all the undelivered letters from his parents. He caressed the papers with his fingers, smearing ink across the faded letters. The paper's rough texture had long ago been worn smooth.

"Why don't you answer my letters?" Pedro mumbled as he clenched a letter so tight that it became a sweat-smeared wad. "I miss you, Mamá and Papá," he said, flattening the letters the best he could. He then stowed them back into the satchel. "Mamá and Papá, you would like my new family and friends in Rose. Everything *must* work out okay with my farm and with you at home. God bless you."

Pedro blew the candle out and turned toward the star-filled heavens. All the stars overhead reminded him of all his caring friends in Rose, who watched over him and provided a guiding light. *It is hard for Pedro to be sad when surrounded by such caring friends*, he thought.

A peaceful smile grew on Pedro's face. He sat there in silence watching the full-moon shadows dance as the wind played with the branches. Besides watching moon shadows, Pedro kept an eye out for pickle poachers and for his pickle blossoms to set.

An additional week of waiting under the persimmon tree brought no further pickle progress. During idle moments, Pedro wrote letters to loved ones back on the Chaco Plain—writing more this week than he had any previous week since coming to America. During this waiting, Pedro even wrote his brothers—anything to get word of his mother and father. He not only wanted to know they were healthy and safe, but now that he had money, he wanted to wire them money. *That would be something*, Pedro thought. *For a change, I can send Mamá and Papá money.*

Idle times also brought distant painful memories, and nearby worries. *Why haven't I heard from Mamá and Papá?* Pedro stressed. *I've also not heard from Mr. Jim. What is wrong with me?* Pedro spent much idle time wondering. *Am I not a good son? A good American?*

On one especially idle afternoon, Pedro began the long walk into town. The scorching sun and his blistering neck were the least of Pedro's worries. His growth as an American, the health and safety of his parents, and the goodness of his soul all weighed on his thoughts, even above pickle plant worries—although, this was worry enough. "When will my pickle plants set pickles?" Pedro shouted into the desiccating wind. Deep down, Pedro knew the answer.

"I am doing something wrong," Pedro said to himself under the afternoon sun, as he adjusted what was left of his collar to cover as many blisters as possible. *Jim will know what to do*, Pedro thought as his knobby knees worked overtime to close in on the last kilometer leading into Rose.

Pedro expected to find Jim at his old bench at The Yellow Rose. Since he didn't walk into town often these days, he planned to not only talk with Jim about pickles but also drop off a package to Fred on this particular trip. The drop-off place was close to the store. Pedro figured it would be better to drop the special package off first and only then find Mr. Jim.

Pedro had long ago lost count of how many walks he had made into town. This one was no different than all the others, except the sky seemed distant and lonely. No vultures riding thermals on such a warm day got Pedro wondering. *What happened to them all?* Pedro corrected himself in thought: *This walk is different. For one, the juniper air is much too pale. What is going on with the juniper?*

Still one vulture-less kilometer from town and one kilometer from Jim's help, Pedro noticed a white car speeding toward him. The siren's wail momentarily took Pedro's attention from wilting plants, blistering neck, straining little legs, and sun-scalded knobby knees protruding through torn jeans. The car and dust cloud would reach Pedro in seconds. It wasn't just any car. It was the sheriff's patrol car. Pedro stepped far off the road to allow it to speed past. Instead, the patrol car skidded to a stop, sending dust all over Pedro's ratted hair. Pedro held the special package tight in twitching fingers.

As the deputy got out, a confused Pedro asked, "What is the matter, sir?"

The deputy shouted things Pedro didn't understand. He then ran up to Pedro and grabbed his wrist. Twisting hard, he sent Pedro face-first into the dusty road. The special package was flung off somewhere behind a Spanish dagger yucca growing beyond the road shoulder. The deputy handcuffed Pedro and shackled him into the back of the patrol car.

The deputy collected all the stuff Pedro had been carrying. Among the rocks, he found and opened Pedro's special package, but not without first photographing everything and carefully inventorying evidence. He counted ten bags of white powder in it—and it wasn't pickle pollination powder.

As the deputy sped down the road back to the sheriff's office, he looked at Pedro in the rearview mirror and said, "Hey, greaseball, you thought you would get away with this? This ain't Mexico or wherever dipshit town or country you come from. This is America. We don't tolerate your kind coming here and bringing your toilet with you."

Although Pedro didn't understand most of what the deputy said, he knew enough about police to realize he was in deep trouble. No one told Pedro anything, and throughout the entire police interrogation, Pedro did just what Leonard had told him to do—he remained silent. The silence brought out worries he'd never thought he would ever know. *Will I never see my farm again? Mamá and Papá? Mr. Jim's idle bench moments? Will I never again pull waxed paper off Anna Maria's gift meats? Will I no longer smell junipers? Join cactus wrens in song? Experience moonlit raggedness? No more thoughtful moments under the persimmon tree? No more comforts of home?*

The interrogation room's sights and smells were foreign to Pedro. *This is not America.* Pedro sulked as the interrogator droned away. After the droning stopped, more police led Pedro toward his cell. Pedro crinkled his nose, lowered his eyes, and slowed his pace during the long walk into the shadowy unknown.

Interactions in Pedro's short and sheltered life had offered him only sweet desserts—dulce de mamón smothered in extra-sugar syrup. He had never truly known life's full palette or senses. He'd not known the acrid taste of defeat or the plummeting sound a soul makes as it hits rock bottom. However, once exposed to life's full palette of senses, no one, least of all Pedro, could turn the clock back—he knew that dulce de mamóns would never taste as sweet again.

Confused more than ever, Pedro sat in the jail cell, trying to make sense of what had happened. The old and new smells that wafted into Pedro's cell seemed to slow the clock's ticking, which came from somewhere beyond his field of vision.

Two women officers saved Pedro from the smells, the ticking, and the taunts from all the surrounding cells as they led him down to the courthouse, where he learned he was to stand trial for drug smuggling. Pedro remained silent throughout the officers' many long questions. His thoughts jumped faster than a jararaca strike. *How are Mamá and Papá doing? What was that smell? Who is going to water my pickle plants? I can still hear the ticking clock. Am I still in America? What did he mean drugs? I want my persimmon tree. I want a tereré. Where is Jim?*

Pedro heard the officers say something about remaining silent. Pedro recalled this was what Leonard had also told him to do. Pedro didn't find remaining silent hard. No matter how hard Pedro tried to ask questions, nothing came out. He remained silent. The only words Pedro was able to make were to ask for Jim. He asked several times. Jim never came.

Pedro tried to ask for a translator, but the words also came out so jumbled that no one knew what he said—or they didn't care. Despite his troubled mind, Pedro found a little solace and strength in being an American and in owning a real and honest-to-God American farm.

"Americans protect their own kind, after all," Pedro said as he waited for his translator. Besides, Pedro had an unwavering faith in Americans and the American justice system. *Where is Mr. Jim?* Lingering cell odors drifted from Pedro's clothes into the courthouse as he waited for Jim, the translator, and an explanation—of everything.

When the court-appointed translator arrived, Pedro began understanding the judge's instructions. However, he needed no translation to understand what the judge said next. Pedro expected leniency since he still had no idea what he had done or why the deputy arrested him. Stray thoughts swarmed through Pedro's head as the magistrate, using plain-enough words, pointed at Pedro and said, "We don't like your kind in these parts. You're facing a possible two-year confinement in prison. Guards, please escort this scum out of my courtroom."

With that, the guards led Pedro away from the courtroom, away from the spectacle, and away from the American dream. As the camarero described it, the guards led Pedro down that silent one-way corridor built specifically for Pedros the world over. To the camarero, it was a foregone conclusion. It had always been Pedro's destiny—the moment he had left the Chaco Plain.

7

Exactly two months later, Jim was sitting on his bench, alternating between twirling and smoothing out his freshly cleaned and degreased Stetson. As Simon finished with his last customer in what had been a long line, he shouted across the store, "Hey, Jim! How's that nice little new pecan grove you and Harry went in together on? You must have five acres—and they look mighty sharp."

"Nah, it's only four acres, but they're doing fabulous," Jim said. Things are looking up this year—everything worked out just right. If that corporation buys me out, at least my farm and orchard will be worth that much more—I'll get top dollar."

As another customer walked up to the counter, Simon blurted, "It worked out just as you said it would."

With a nod and a sharp chuckle, Jim chimed in, "Yeah, it never would have worked out so well if it weren't for that naïve immigrant boy."

"Wasn't his name Peppy?"

"Whatever."

By the time the camarero began closing the cantina for the night, the farmer had become less intoxicated but more, much more, tired. It had been a long day—for both of them. Besides the farmer, the camarero served only one other customer the whole night—and he came in just as the camarero wound down his Pedro story. It was too late for more serving, talking, or storytelling. The camarero asked both weary patrons to leave so he could close.

As the farmer staggered for the door, the camarero turned to him and asked, "What do you think of Pedro's story? Do you still want to go to America now that you've heard how Americans treat poor people from the Chaco Plain?"

"I've had enough drunken thoughts for one night," the farmer said. "I gotta head home—I have to get up early and head back into the fields. If I'm going to make a go of it, I guess I have to start sometime. Tomorrow is just as good as the next day."

After the farmer staggered beyond earshot, the other customer, who wore faded military fatigues that hid his current occupation and status in life, said to the camarero, "I overheard the ending of your Pedro story. Why didn't you tell him the truth about Pedro?"

"What do you mean?" the camarero said to his serious-minded patron. "I told him Pedro's story just the way it happened. I should know—I *do* know. I've told Pedro's story dozens of times before. Are you saying you know it differently or could tell it better?"

"Sure, I can, 'cause you got it all wrong. I should know. Pedro was a friend of one of my cousins. So, I know Pedro's true story, clearly better than you."

The camarero was tired, but not too tired to hear something new about Pedro's life, even if it was just a preposterous lie. He pulled down two barstools and motioned for the stranger to sit back down.

"Pedro was not as naïve or simpleminded as you made him out to be," the stranger said. "He is, after all, from the Chaco Plain. We are too sharp to be so easily fooled as *your* Pedro. The real Pedro fooled the Pittsylvania County Americans, not the other way around. Americans are easily swayed by their prejudice, conceit, and ignorance."

"On that, you and I both agree," chimed in the camarero.

"Yes, of course. Americans always look down on us, but we should look down on them," he said as if he was about to spit on the cantina's floor. "Pedro knew this, so he cunningly manipulated the naïve Americans in Pittsylvania County."

"Are you saying the Americans didn't take advantage of innocent and naïve Pedro?"

"They tried to, and thought they were, but Pedro wasn't naïve—he had other plans and always stayed one step ahead of the Americans. You see, besides having an expanded pecan orchard and the strongest new fence Pittsylvania County had ever seen, Rose would soon have a new property owner—and a new boss."

The camarero didn't know what the stranger was saying or implying. Still, he was intrigued enough to ask him to continue his gripping fictional tale. Both weary men ignored the clock and the moon's long arc across the Chaco Plain's ink-black sky. They swapped and reswapped Pedro stories and happenings that they both fervently believed to be true.

"Pedro was not as poor or naïve as he led on, or as you tell it," the stranger repeated to the camarero.

"What are you talking about? Of course, he was a poor immigrant—that is why he left the Chaco Plain and went through his terrible ordeal to travel to America."

"He was *not* poor. He only pretended to be—but a poor, helpless sap is all Americans see in any immigrant. That is what they wanted to see."

"That makes sense," the camarero added as the stranger retook his seat.

"We Guaraní are much too smart to be preyed upon by ignorant people—we Guaraní are *not* gullible," the stranger said as they leaned toward one another. "As it turned out," the stranger added, "the international corporation buying up land and farms in Pittsylvania County to build the new casino was owned by no other than Pedro."

"Oh, sir, I believe you are making fun of me. It is much too late, and we are both too tired to spring such practical jokes. Do you think I would believe any foolish thing you tell me? You would have me believe poor Pedro owned an international corporation that built luxury resorts and casinos? I may be a poor camarero, but I'm no fool."

"Why not? Pedro is from the Chaco Plain, is he not? The world's brightest minds and smartest people come from the Chaco Plain—no? We beat the mighty Bolivian army in the Chaco War. We outsmarted the simple, arrogant townsfolk of Pittsylvania County. Why can't we be the owner of a successful business? Besides, I know this of Pedro. This is the true Pedro, not the make-believe poor immigrant cliché version you peddle."

"If he was so rich, why pretend to be a poor immigrant?" the camarero asked while leaning toward the entertaining stranger.

"This makes perfect sense to me. If it doesn't to you, you must *not* be from the Chaco Plain. You're not from Uruguay, are you? We Paraguayans have our wits and smarts."

"I am a Guaraní," the camarero said.

Ignoring the camarero's defensiveness, the stranger said, "If you owned a corporation and wanted to invest in a community, wouldn't you want to know the real character of its residents?" The camarero just sat there staring. Trying another tack, the stranger added, "This is like that fairyland story of the medieval English king who walks throughout his kingdom dressed as a peasant." The stranger slowly rose from his chair, and the camarero shifted in his seat. "If Pedro rode into town in a limousine and then strutted up a red carpet emblazoned with ribbons and accompanied by the town's brass band in all its glory, do you think the Americans would present an accurate picture of who they were? Who they were deep in their hearts?"

"I guess not—I guess that makes sense. Still ..."

"Sure, it does. You must have a little Gran Chaco in you after all—more than I thought moments ago," the stranger said as he flashed a toothy grin. "Pedro just wandered into town pretending to be a humble working-class immigrant as poor as the baby Jesus. His plan ended there. The rest of Pedro's image grew organically by the true nature of the Rosarians. They conjured the rest, and Pedro just played along. In truth, Pedro was a multimillionaire. He earned his wealth by owning Paraguay's largest tannin factory. The townsfolk of Rose learned the truth of their new financial benefactor only from a letter sent to all Rosarians by corporate president Petre Ortez, otherwise known as Pedro."

After hearing that story, the camarero burst out in laughter. With a smile not seen in a long time, he sputtered, "If true, I bet the people of Rose had a lot of explaining to do—all those ignorant people pretended to be his friend. They thought they were preying on the weak and inferior. The laugh was on them …" The camarero paused as if pondering a life-changing event. He looked at the wall-mounted clock and then gazed outside the window. The first glimpse of dawn hit the few scattered buildings, and the distant savannah expanse was visible from the cantina's frost-tinted window. "I'm not sure if any of what you just said about Pedro is true, but I found your tale amusing. I now need to lock up and head home."

After the confused camarero and strange customer said their thanks and goodbyes, the weary men walked home—in separate directions. On his way home, the stranger briskly passed one decrepit building after another. In some perverse way, the moon's reflection off broken window shards and ragged glass fragments brought to the stranger's mind a hopeful future. *We Guaraní are bright, strong, and resourceful, just like Pedro. We will be great again*, thought the stranger as he neared the last leg of his walk home.

The camarero's long drift home also provided him time to think. Each hovel and falling-down shanty he passed brought back fond memories of its former occupants—families who were once friends, neighbors, and relatives. He passed more than a few once-lovely homes that showed signs of the savannah reclaiming ownership, but the camarero's memories refused to budge. His modest home was straight ahead. The rusty hinges that creaked on the wobbly gate overwhelmed his heavy sigh as he thought, *If Pedro was a rich business owner, he certainly didn't come from this poor corner of the Chaco Plain.*

8

Jim's memorial service reception took place in Rose's most luxurious public building, the town's new community center. Nearly everyone from town had come to pay their respects to Jim. He died two weeks earlier of a massive heart attack while giving an orchard tour to a visiting Boy Scout troop. He collapsed right next to a row of pecan seedlings that Pedro had planted.

The large turnout for both the funeral and reception indicated how much everyone liked Jim, not only as a person but also as a proud humanitarian. He always lent a helping hand to anyone in need. Every Rosarian Pedro knew had turned up, including Simon, Harry, Kyle, the barber, the town's entire police force, the chamber of commerce, the Rotarians, and the entire civic pride committee. The high school band played Jim's favorite numbers in the parking lot. Except for Pedro, all Rosarians were there, including Jim's weeping, black-veiled wife.

The civic pride committee president rose from his seat from the back of the community center to announce the committee's recent decision. "In light of Jim's untimely passing and his great humanitarianism, the committee commissioned a bronze statue. It will be a likeness of Jim sitting on his favorite bench, the one over at The Yellow Rose." The Rosarians filled the community center with applause—much too vigorous for such a solemn occasion.

After the cheers died down, the civic pride committee president announced that the plan was to have the statue of Jim, Stetson in hand, "looking cheery-eyed at kids playing in the store's chicken feed aisle." In his noble praise for Jim's virtues, the president continued addressing the crowd. "Jim, besides being a true patriot and a true friend, was the heart and soul of Rose—God's country."

The audience clapped and whistled as if the local high school football team had just won the regional championship.

"I will sorely miss him," Simon mused, while pushing back a tear. "He was a good friend. I'll miss our talks. I can't even remember if we had the bench before he took it as his own. With his statue just a-sittin' on the bench, like Jim had done for so many years, maybe when it's slow in the store, I'll occasionally keep on talking to Jim. Me a-talkin' and he just sitting—it'll be like old times."

Before the applause and murmuring subsided, Jim's wife, also a member of the civic pride committee, stood up, pushed back her veil, and began sharing fond memories of her dear Jim. She not only shared humorous stories of their good times, but she retold a story that most in Rose already knew but were more than willing to hear again and again. While she was singing Jim's praises, Pedro's name came up on more than one occasion.

"I know you all are aware of Jim's kind heart and civic-mindedness." She paused long enough for everyone to nod their approval, and a couple of amens echoed off the community center walls. "As a perfect example of Jim's kind and warm heart, I'm sure many of you remember that poor immigrant kid, Peppy, whom Jim befriended." An even louder applause erupted as she smiled and turned back to her congregation, not unlike a hell-and-brimstone Baptist preacher.

Someone in the crowd shouted out, "The pickle guy!" The crowd's laughs and cheers reached a new crescendo as if the high school football team had just won the Super Bowl.

Jim's wife motioned the crowd to settle down. "Many ordinary Americans would simply have ignored Peppy and his poor immigrant needs—but not Jim!"

"No, not Jim!" someone from the back roared.

"Jim was no innkeeper who cast Joseph and Mary and the forthcoming baby Jesus outside on a stormy night. No, Jim took poor Peppy under his wing and helped him in ways only a good Christian would. That only my dear Jim would. Not only did he clothe him, shelter him, and feed the wretched immigrant, but he showed this ignorant boy the ropes of how to plant and care for pecan trees. Jim even leased some of his land to Peppy. He always had such a soft spot for the poor and unfortunate." She closed her sermon by sharing a humorous story about Jim helping Peppy—the poor immigrant child. "As you all know, Jim had quite the wicked sense of humor."

"Amen!" someone shouted deep within the congregation.

"It turns out that Jim's sense of humor even rubbed off on the wretched immigrant. The two of them, Jim and Peppy, became fast friends and joked around with each other. For instance, I'm sure many of you remember, but Jim and Peppy had this inside joke that they bantered back and forth. As Jim taught Peppy the ways of pecan farming, the two of them joked about imagining the pecan trees as pickle plants. Imagine the absurdity of that, master and apprentice having fun planting pecans together while sharing an ever-escalating series of absurd jokes and carefree imaginations."

After a long pause, she mused, "I sure do miss Jim, my soul mate. And it's too bad that Peppy fell back on his immigrant ways and resorted to drug dealing and other illegal doings. It nearly broke Jim's heart when he heard the news of Peppy's arrest. I told Jim more than once, 'You did all you could—but some people simply can't be helped, no matter how hard you try. It's in their very nature.' However, being a good Christian, Jim tried and tried to save that wretched Peppy.

"Trying to help that no-good immigrant was only one of the many kindhearted things Jim has done over the years," she continued. "Therefore, I can think of no better tribute to this great man than having a bronze statue made in his likeness. He would have liked that."

As she walked down from the pulpit, returned to her seat, and returned the veil over her face, the congregation roared, whistled, shouted, and threw out more *amens* on top of each other. It was livelier than any traditional fire-and-brimstone Southern Baptist sermon that West Texas had ever seen.

Those who met Pedro or told his stories may never discover the truth about him because we live in a complex world, and as such, truth remain elusive. However, if they wanted to, they could easily uncover additional factual information on Pedro and his earlier life and experiences since original sources still remained.

There were rumors that blood relatives lived not far from Pedro's childhood home on the Chaco Plain. If anyone bothered to look for living family members, they would have found someone claiming to be Pedro's brother. He whiled away his time in his hometown cantina, telling Pedro stories to his camarero. This camarero was a man who had also lived his entire adult life in the same hovel. If someone bothered to ask either man about Pedro, they would have had choice words to say about him, the younger and more storied brother.

It would not have taken much prompting for his brother to talk about Pedro. It was his favorite topic after he had too many cañas or Pilsen La Rosas—sometimes La Negras, depending upon his mood. When the man was drunk, he told the story of his good-for-nothin' little brother, who abandoned his family, homeland, and culture to sneak off to America without a word.

According to his brother's drunken tales, Pedro stole their mamá and papá's life savings.

Shortly after Pedro turned his back on his mamá and papá, a drug overlord attacked the family and sent them scattering throughout the Chaco savannah. Weakened by hunger and poverty, they were no match for the gangs as they swept through the area preying on the weak and vulnerable. The Chaco Plain hadn't seen such violence and chaos since Operation Condor, the American-backed torture program unleashed throughout Paraguay in the 1970s and '80s.

The drunken Guaraní often spat tobacco juice on the floor whenever forced to say his little brother's name. "Mamá died because of him!" he shouted at anyone who listened. According to the often-inebriated older brother, their mother "died of broken finances, a broken back, broken heart, and broken spirit—all because of Pedro."

While it didn't take much to get him started, no regular cantina patron ever asked him about Pedro because they had heard the story before, repeatedly. They didn't need to hear it again. They also didn't need to have their shoes spat on again. No one from beyond the village ever came by and prompted him because everyone was content with *their* version of Pedro. Why shake firmly held core beliefs and worldviews with a bit of truth and understanding?

Almost no one looked for Pedro—not any more than West Texans looked for wild persimmon trees. Rumors had it that Pedro had died in prison. Some claimed the Border Patrol had sent him to Mexico, where he died a victim of drug violence. Rumors circulated that he escaped prison and was living somewhere in Bolivia. If someone probed deeply around Pedro's hometown, they might have found relatives. Each had their own unreliable stories to tell and ideologies to reinforce, champion, and radicalize. The faithful and patriotic Chaco Plain old guard claimed Pedro's father was still alive and running a quebracho tree harvest and tannin factory deep in the Bolivian Chaco Plain.

As this storyline went, it was Pedro's father who planned and paid for the raids and the ransacking of the poor villages throughout the borderland and disputed regions of the Chaco Plain. They claimed this same quebracho tree harvest and tannin factory was responsible for the lion's share of the deforestation that had occurred throughout the region. They claimed those same processes were driving more villages and families into poverty.

The old-timers lamented modern-day life on the savannah—times were not as they used to be on the Chaco Plain. They felt deep within their bones that Pedro's family empire was at the epicenter of those life-changing storms. The same type of storms that continued to grow and rake across the southern continent's poverty-stricken prairies, playas, and plains.

9

Sharon was the closest anyone came to finding the real Pedro. Sharon, the wanderer, the seeker of the real America. This understanding came not only from the weeks she and Charley spent with Pedro but also from the many weeks she searched for him on her return trip to Minnesota.

After delivering Pedro's note to Jim, Sharon and Charley spent the next few months exploring the people, places, and faces of America, throughout California, the mountain states, and the Pacific Northwest. She'd met many souls on her journey, but none as memorable as Pedro. Lonely roadways often got her thinking, *I wonder what Pedro is up to now. How is his farm making out? Is he okay?* It was along Idaho's Snake River Plain, east of

Hell's Half Acre, that she decided to put her worries to rest. She and Charley turned south toward Texas. South toward Pedro. Besides, they didn't need to return to Minnesota anytime soon.

Upon arriving back in West Texas, bone-jarring waves of regret swept through her after she found no signs of Pedro's whereabouts. *I should've come back and checked on him*, she thought. *Did help ever arrive?* She would now never know.

There has to be some indication where he went, Sharon fretted as she and Charley searched along the empty rows of the young pecan grove, through the scattered remains of the thatched lean-to, and next to the persimmon stump. For the longest time, Sharon stared at the sunlight glistening off persimmon sap still oozing from the freshly severed trunk. *Who would cut down Pedro's persimmon tree?* No clues remained—there was only a stiff wind and indifferent vultures circling high overhead.

Sharon and Charley took Pedro's well-worn path into Rose. Hoping someone would know what happened to Pedro, Sharon began asking anyone she met on the streets and in the shops—throughout the entire town. She also asked for Jim but found only a stiff and cold statue perched on a bench. No one beyond Anna Maria said they knew Pedro much at all.

"Ever since the officers arrested Pedro, I regretted a thousand times not doing more to help him—the poor soul," Anna Maria confessed.

Sharon and Charley took up temporary residence in Anna Maria's back room. During this time together, they swapped Pedro stories—Sharon to find a way to find Pedro, and Anna Maria to reassure herself that she wasn't partly to blame. Anna Maria also needed to figure out if what the townsfolk said had happened really *had* happened. Sharon increasingly spent time alone. She needed to think long and hard. Despite all the effort to uncover the truth, in the end, Sharon knew something wasn't quite right, but she couldn't find words to describe how she felt.

Based on different stories, backgrounds, and world-views, Sharon understood that she might never know the true Pedro. She thought she had. As time progressed, guilt replaced truisms, and doubt replaced guilt. *Had there ever been a Pedro?* she pondered. *Did I fabricate him in my mind? Was I the one with the fever?* While she searched for answers in Rose, Sharon had a lot of time to ruminate on her many solo wanderings. *Dreams are not the only powerful forces conjured from a person's mind,* she imagined. *So too are self-serving needs and arrogance.*

"Maybe everyone needed a good Pedro story, whether true or not," Sharon once speculated to Anna Maria.

After a long pause, in which Anna Maria sat silent while continually trying to press straight, nonexistent wrinkles in her flower-printed linen blouse, Sharon added, "Whether true or not—it doesn't really matter. Does it?"

"It seemed obvious people were taking advantage of Pedro," Anna Maria blurted. "What did I do? I just sat silent and gave him a handout every once in a while—"

"What was I reaching for?" Sharon interrupted, but the words trailed off into the silence of her thoughts. "Maybe that's why I left home to search for the real America."

As Sharon talked, Anna Maria sat silent, wondering, *If Sharon was so into searching, why didn't she come back and search for Pedro when he needed her?*

If Sharon had known what Anna Maria, and the other tellers of Pedro stories, had been thinking, she likely would have told them, "If we all are truly honest with ourselves, we would conclude that there's no surer way to quiet what stirs deep within us than to firm up long and closely held perceptions and rally around the like-minded." Sharon thought on that a moment, before getting up and walking off, leaving Anna Maria alone with her thoughts.

Sharon continued her reflections as she wandered Rose's empty streets, back alleys, and closed storefronts.

It was as if the heavy evening air kept everyone inside. Using words she imagined Jim could relate to, Sharon likened her ruminations to a fresh coat of barn paint masking soft beetle-chewed wood. Intuitively, she knew that Pedro—not Pedro the person, but Pedro the larger-than-life symbol—represented many things across the vast American expanse. *As soon as Pedro, real or imagined, began searching for the American dream,* she visualized, *he nicked the barn's thin veneer, exposing its underlying soft and swelling underbelly. From that moment on, the barn's fate was set.*

Moon-shadowed alleyways greeted Sharon on her remaining Rose wanderings, as they darted back and forth between footstep and mind, and back again. It was the perfect backdrop for both clarity and thoughtful reflection ...

All he wanted was a little slice of the American Dream— just a slice. Was that too much to ask? she pondered. Her mind and memories hung limp from both the gravity and oppressive air. The moon shadows faded into the night as she continued her silent rants into farther reaches of her stroll.

Sharon's thoughts coalesced faster than a Texas summer thunderhead. Through this nicked veneer came an outpouring of pent-up anxiety and swollen discontent. If she had thought about it harder, she might have realized that this discontent was larger than the great savannah, larger than Paraguay, and larger than West Texas itself. Certainly larger than the mere skin-and-bones, knobby-kneed little Pedro from the Chaco Plain.

If Sharon searched far and wide for the real Pedro, she might have gotten into the head of a lone stranger whiling away his time in a distant cantina and heard him say, "When times get hard, we all need a little comfort to ease troubled minds. Some worries are too deep for the soothing powers of a mere tereré—or two."

If Sharon had visited this distant cantina, she would likely have found the lone stranger wasn't often alone anymore. She would've discovered that he and the local camarero had become fast friends. Sharon would likely have joined them in their many late-night philosophizing debates—if she'd had the opportunity. All three would have known all too well that thoughtful reflection was rare in such troubled times.

Through Sharon's philosophizing ramblings, both near and far, and even the imagined, she began realizing Pedro was real enough. Real enough to her and real enough to Anna Maria. Real enough not to be reduced to a cultural cliché or a nameless caricature. If she wandered farther, she would have found Pedro was also real enough to the desperate and suffering Chaco Plain camarero, who needed just a little hope and pride to get him through trying times. Sharon also understood that Pedro was real enough to the good people of Rose as they went about reinforcing community spirit and their faith in Rosarian goodness.

Through her wanderings, Sharon began understanding that there's a little Pedro in everyone. But lying deep within us was also a little Jim, Harry, Kyle, Rosarian civic pride committee, camarero, and dysfunctional sibling. She didn't need a camarero's story or a rousing Rosarian sermon to know a desperate person will believe anything as long as it makes their life simpler and provides them with a little solace. She began to understand that it takes only one person to plant a wayward seed or sprig. The next thing the unsuspecting person would know is that they had bought the entire farm.

She imagined that whatever the farm eventually becomes would depend not just on what wayward seed was planted. *Depending on who waters, nourishes, or provides comfort to the sprout, widely different species may end up flourishing*, she pondered. While wandering Rose's empty streets, she realized blossoms tended by a kind-hearted soul, like Pedro, may set entirely different fruit than one tended to by someone like Leonard. In the end, if luck would have it, a person may find themselves eating pecan pie at a Rosarian church picnic—where all is good in the world. While pecan pie may not compare with the sweetness of dulce de mamón, it is a far cry from the backroom table that serves only pickles.

"Pedro never once had a choice—or a chance," she said out loud as she stopped in her tracks outside The Yellow Rose. If only Sharon had begun her search for the real America a few months earlier than she had, she might have overheard Simon's prophetic remark to Pedro, "We Americans love pickles."

ABOUT THE AUTHOR

David Ek has a Master of Science degree in geoscience. He held a successful and award-winning career with the National Park Service, where he led science and natural resources teams throughout the country. During these local, regional, and national resource challenges, David wrote extensively for science and management audiences and the general public.

On the literary side, David writes both fiction and nonfiction. Editors for literary journals have found his writing "strong" with "much to admire." His short stories have appeared in *Canary*, "a literary journal of the environmental crisis" and *Weber: The Contemporary West*. Publishers are currently reviewing his various book-length manuscripts.

When not sciencing and writing, David has been an active rock and mountain climber, caver, and explorer of the American wilds. He is currently a member of the Virginia Writers Club and the Pacific Northwest Writers Association.

A native of Seattle, Washington, David has lived and traveled extensively across the country throughout his accumulated years. He currently lives with his wife, children, cat, and dogs in rural northern Virginia.

David is available for select readings and lectures. To inquire about possible appearances, or to learn more about his writings, please visit him online at https://EkDavidAuthor.com.

www.ingramcontent.com/pod-product-compliance
Lightning Source LLC
Chambersburg PA
CBHW040834010826
48978CB00012BB/754